T0132417

JENNIFER PATRICK STEPHENS

Have You Seen My Umbrella?

To order additional copies of this book, contact:
Xlibris
844-714-8691
www.Xlibris.com
Orders@Xlibris.com

ISBN: 978-1-6641-0944-5 (sc)
ISBN: 978-1-6641-0943-8 (e)

Print information available on the last page

Rev. date: 09/29/2021

Have You Seen My Umbrella?

Written by
Illustrations by: Joshua Bonneau

On a misty, cloudy, rainy day, Sarah decided to take her umbrella for a walk.

Splash! Splash! She was having fun jumping into the water puddles.

While dancing in the rain, a strong wind came by and whirled her umbrella away.

"OHH NO!" she cried. Where did her dear umbrella have gone?

Sarah sat down on the log. She asked the frog leaping from lily pad to lily pad. “Have you seen my umbrella?” she asked. “No not I,” said the frog.

Sarah walked down the path and ran into a pasture of calf. “Have you seen my umbrella?” she asked. “No not I,” said the calf.

She then came to an old creaking gate. To her surprise she saw a slithering snake sliding down the pole. “Have you seen my umbrella?” she asked. “No not I,” said the snake.

Skipping along Sarah approached a farmer. "Have you seen my umbrella?" she asked. "I think you are getting a little warmer. I seen it floating near by," said the farmer.

Over the hill Sarah went with excitement in her eyes. She saw a cat tangled in yarn. "Have you seen my umbrella?" she asked. "Why, yes it's near the lake," he yawned.

Sarah ran to the lake. She saw it laying on its side.

"There you are. I found you," she cried.

Printed in the United States
by Baker & Taylor Publisher Services